Ruben Kane (R.K)

By

Eddie J Martin

I0675507

For: Kenneth Martin, my grandson.

We never know what life has in store for us,

We just have to roll with the punches.

You've become one hell of a man, I'm proud of you.

A Message from the Author

I've always dreamed for as long as I can remember, I believe it's good to dream especially if you have stress or depression in your life. Dreams take you to another time and place other than the one you're in, better than the one you're in (hopefully). And you can be anyone you want to be, go anywhere you want to go, it's your dream. So go on and dream.

Cleveland Ohio, summer 1938. Gas was nineteen-cents a gallon and a meal was a $.80, including the tip. Pint of wine was forty-nine cents and a fifth of whiskey$1.75. Life was good. Until my wife's lover was murdered and the cops suspected her, that's where I came in.

A wife, a girlfriend, a murdered boyfriend and a gay lover. It don't get any more complicated than that.

R.K. (Ruben Kane)

PROLOGUE

Ruben Kane have just gotten smoother, he was picking

up his girlfriend to go out on a dinner date that night,

nice jazz music, maybe some dancing and back to the

house for some heavy sex. Then he

learned his wife's boyfriend had just been murdered

and the police have arrested her.

Will a murder charge bring Ruben and his

wife Ella back together, after all they been

going their separate ways for a year or

more.

Why there're still living together

neither one really Knows, something about strange bedfellows except they have separate bedrooms. They do meet over coffee and the daily newspaper in the morning when both are at home. This morning she wasn't home and he made his own coffee and read the paper just like always. He thought maybe this morning he'd stop off at the local diner before he went to the office. I'm what you call, a go to guy, if you're in trouble you come to me. Some people call me a detective but I don't have a license (right now) it's a long story. I do have a 38 Smith and Wesson pistol and a half fifth bottle of Jim Bean in my desk drawer. So yes, I've got everything I need to take care of business. Next stop Skippy's Diner for breakfast.

After ham and eggs, grits, toast and coffee I was ready to start the day. I got back in my 1938

Buick, start it up, check the gas tank level and headed for the office. My office is in the Stanford building, downtown Cleveland Ohio. 20 stories high, I'm on the 13th floor. If I had to pay for this place I wouldn't be able to visit, but as it stands I pay zero in rent. I did a job once for this banker and his family, he had this office space and I needed an office so WA La, here I am.

CHAPER 1

I walked in the office and damn, there was my Sec., Rita. I never expect her to get in before me but ten in the morning and there she was. Rita is of Mexican descent who is an illegal in the country and has been here some three years now. She's been working for me for eighteen months. At 5 foot five and just as wide, 26 years old, long black hair, cute face and talk plenty

shit.

Good morning R.K., and how are you this fine day?

Rita said.

Uh Oh. The warm welcome means it's either pay day

and I forgot or she got laid last night.

I'm doing fine Rita, and how are you? You seem to be

in a good mood this morning, I said.

I am she said, I had a night to remember. Dinner,

dancing and lots of sex. Would you like to hear about

it?

I would not Rita, save it for your memoirs I said. Any

messages?

Well you got one call from your policy guy, he said

your numbers didn't come out last night and you owe

him 8 bucks. He'll be over later on today to collect. And

some chick by the name of Dolores call and said to tell

you, let me get this straight now, that the welcome mat
is no longer out for you. Are you ready for your coffee
Rita said?

Lay it on me, I just need to spice it up a little. I threw
my fedora on the hat rack, took my sport coat off and
Hung that behind my chair. Sat down and put my feet
up on the desk and took my bottle of Jim bean out of
the bottom drawer, poured two fingers in my coffee
cup and took a sip. Nice! Theo's old boys down there in
Kentucky show know how to make some good whiskey.
 When the phone rang Rita answered it with; Ruben
Kane Detective agency, Rita speaking. Oh hello Mrs.
Kane, yes he's here hold on.
Mr. K, your wife's on line 1.
 I don't know why she always say that because we only
have the one line. Makes her feel important I guess.

Yes Ella, I said.

Ruben, I'm in jail and I need your help. I only have this one phone call so listen. I'm going to need a Bail bondsman and a lawyer.

You want to tell me why you're in jail Ella?

I'm in jail for murder Ruben, murder! Then she bust out crying. I didn't do it, I didn't do it.

Calm down Ella, calm down, now tell me what happened.

Ruben I only have a few minutes so I don't have time to tell you the whole story, just get me a lawyer and a bail bondsman and get me the hell out of here. I can't take this place any longer.

Okay Ella sit tight and I'll have someone right down there.

T.K. Lofts was a lawyer I use from time to time, small Jewish man in his early 50s. Horn-rimmed glasses, dark suit with vest and bowtie, always wears his black fedora and Freemans high top shoes. Typical lawyer. Pretty good at what he does, at least I haven't stayed in jail for very long with him on the job.

The bondsman, Willis Moore, he was another fellow I went to school with although he was a few years ahead of me and my crowd and went a totally different direction. He told me once that if we were so bent on doing the wrong thing then there should be someone around to Bail us out and that's why he became a bondsman. He gets a lot of business, mine included. So I call Willis and told him about Ella and he said he'd get right over there being only two blocks from the jail, He'd make it there before me.

I poured another two fingers of Jim Bean and thought, Ella in jail for murdering her boyfriend, must be that guy I saw her with in the club. That relationship show turn to shit quickly. Well they say love/hate relationships... But then again I may be jumping the gun or the cops are. I don't see Ella killing anybody but I guess she's capable just as anyone would be depending on the situation. I'll just have to go down to the jail and get her out and find out what this is all about. I never thought I'd be starting the day like this, and I bet I want even get paid.

When I got there the lawyer had been there and gone, Willis and Ella was sitting in the break room talking. Bout time you got here Ella said, shows how much you care about me.

Hold on Ella don't be jumping in my ass, my girlfriend is alive and well so just keep your panties on.

Hello Willis, what's the damage?

Seventy five dollars this time Ruben and T.K. wants to see you in his office as soon as possible.

Ella started crying again and I told her to calm down and let's go grab a cup of coffee.

The diner right around the corner was where all the cops, jailers, lawyers and people out of the courthouse go. It was right at 1 o'clock and a lot of the lunch crowd was still there but we managed to find a booth for two. After we ordered, coffee and a ham and cheese sandwich for me, Ella said that she couldn't eat anything so she just had an iced tea.

Now, I said. You want to tell me what happened that landed you in jail?

Ruben, I know things haven't been just right between us and that may have been partly my fault but also partly yours to. So when it was evident that things wasn't going to get any better I thought a friend for me would be appropriate so that's what I did, got me a friend. Don't get me wrong Ruben, I still care for you but something's not there anymore, something's missing.

Is that why you stayed I said?

I thought that things could be worse if we wasn't together and it was cheaper to keep you, she said.

Am I supposed to think you for that I said? No, I just want you to understand why I did what I did.

When did you meet this fella and how long have you been seeing him? I said.

I've been seeing Richard about eight months now, I met him at the grocery store. He's single and has his own apartment. Does he work I said?

He's a Dentist here on the west side of Cleveland. Denton Dentistry!

If you been seeing the guy for eight months why haven't you moved in with him?

I don't know she said, it never occurred to me.

So now the guy is dead, how did that happen? Ruben asked?

Ruben, I really don't know. We were at his apartment having a few drinks when we ran out, we flipped a coin to see who would go get more, and I lost. Since the liquor store was just around the corner I decided not to drive. Just a 20 minute walk up and back. So I walked to the store, took me approximately 20 minutes and when I got back I found the door open and Richard sitting on the couch slumped over, dead, a bullet hole through his forehead. A tenant pass by the door looked in and saw me standing over the body and called the police.

Since I was there and no one else I was the only suspect so they took me to jail interrogated me and gave me my one phone call the next day. How much did you tell them before TK got there? Nothing, not much. And then after he got there he stopped the interrogation and Willis showed up with my bail.

Do you have any idea who would want to kill him? I said. Girlfriend, boyfriend, or acquaintance you may know of?

To tell you the truth I never knew many of Richard's friends, we mostly stayed in or went to some out of the way lounge that he knew of.

What about his dental practice or patients, he ever talk about them? I said.

No, nothing, Ella said.

So it seems like all you two had in common was a sexual relationship is that about it? I said.

No! It was more than that, it was more than that. It had to be! I really enjoyed his company.

If you say so, I said. Is that all you can tell me?

Yes Ella said, not much is it? Seems like there should be more for that amount of time we spent together.

Yeah! Whatever, I said.

Fuck you Ruben. You do what you do and it's all right but when it comes to me you got something smart to say.

Look Ella, let's stay on the subject of you and your murdered friend and that you may be going away for a long time if we don't find out who did it. One thing I need to ask you before I get started... did you kill him?

Ruben, if I wasn't a lady and in this diner I'd reach over this table and slap the hell out of you. You know damn well I didn't kill him or anybody else. Why you ask me such a question?

Okay, okay, I had to ask. One never knows. I need to go back to the office and make a few phone calls, see what I can dig up on your dentist friend. Also I need to stop by T.K.'s office to see what he can do for you and how deep you're in. Meanwhile I want you to go home and write down everything you can remember about the good doctor. You can leave out the sexual stuff.

Now, are you going to the home we share together or to the good doctor's place? Ruben said.

The hell with you Ruben, Ella said.

I'll call you later, once I have something. Ruben said.

CHAPTER 2

I called Freda and told her what conspired and that our plans had to be put on hold. She said she understood and to call her after everything was settled.

My next call was to Raymond the Barber, Raymond has been in business for over 25 years and even though his shop was on the east side of town he seems to know what's going on all over Cleveland. Raymond was a hell of a man once, 6 feet five, and 300 pounds mostly fat now that he's in his early 60s but still a hell of a man. Always wears that barbers hat and bifocals. Raymond how's it hanging I said?

 R.K., where the hell have you been, I don't see you over this way much anymore. In fact I haven't seen you since that Tonelli thing over a year ago.

 I'm still here Raymond trying to make a dollar. Look it may not be in the papers yet, since it just happened Saturday night but have you heard anything about a Dentist getting blown away over here on the west side? That's news to me R.K., who was he?

A guy by the name of Richard Denton. He had a practice over here call Denton's dentistry.

No, I haven't heard anything yet but like you said it just happened the other night, I'll keep my ears open and let you know if I hear anything.

R.K. you think you gonnia get Ella off? Rita said.

I don't know Rita, from here it looks like she's really in the shits. I'm headed for T.K.'s office I may not be back before you leave, I may call you later to see if any calls came in if not just leave a message on my desk.

Hi Luria, T.K. free? He sure is Mr. Kane, go on in he's expecting you.

Knock knock Ruben said as he entered T.K.'s office. T.K. was on the phone and put up one finger to inform Ruben. Ruben sat down in one of the overstuffed chairs in front of his desk. Thought for a minute got back up and walked over to the small bar and located a bottle of Jim Beam, grab a glass and the ice bucket, poured two fingers and walked back over to the chair and sat down, starched out and crossed his ankles. Swirl the ice around in his glass and took a sip. T.K. got off the phone and told Ruben to make his self-comfortable why don't you.

 I have Ruben said and I might add you getting low on J.B.

Ella! Let's talk about Ella T.K. said.

Okay Ruben said let's do that.

 Ella is in big trouble, what did she tell you T.K. asked? Ruben told T.K. what Ella told him and said he didn't believe she did it but that's just me.

She told me essentially the same thing but the DA is out to burn someone and they have the bull's-eye on Ella. The good doctor was fairly well known and had a following. Ella was seen standing over the body and no one else was around therefore she's the prime suspect. So Ruben it looks like you've got your work cut out for you, where you gonnia start first?

Damn if I know Ruben said. Beat the bushes I guess, it won't be easy. You want to tell me about this relationship you have with Ella? Besides being married that is.

It's a long story T.K., I'll have to tell you about it sometime.

If we go to trial you do know it'll come out don't you?

Yeah I guess so, let's hope it won't get that far.

My first stop had to be the good doctor's apartment, third floor in the better part of town. I know the cops would still be there but I thought maybe I could pick up a little information. From time to time I had run into a detective or two that I knew and we'd trade information. The usual tape was up and one uniform cop on the door and three detectives were inside, the cop on the door told me to move on but it so happen I knew the older of the detectives and he saw me, came to the door and asked me did I have business there.

I told him about Ella and he let me come in the apartment. Said I could look around, of course the other two officers didn't like that. Detective Jeffries the one that let me through asked me was I going to investigate the murder? I told him due to the circumstances I had to.

You will tell me if you come up with anything want you? Jeffries said.

I sure will, Ruben said. Are there any other suspects? No, said Jeffries, just your wife. After 30 minutes in the apartment learning very little

I started feeling those hunger pains so I thought I'd head for Mama Sue's. A soul food place own by a large grandmother type woman that's been in business for over 20 years and who's food is to die for. Greens, ham hocks, neck bones, cornbread, beans, macaroni and cheese. Potato salad and barbecue ribs. I won't be any good after eating all that, can't wait. I stop by the service station first for some of that high ass gas, it must be at least $.28 now. Maybe they have a sale going on, they do from time to time.

Fill it up RK?

Yeah Robbie, how much is it today?

$.32 RK, it went up a little since the last time you were here.

What the hell you guys trying to do get rich?

That's the way it is RK everything is going up, next week it may be as high as $.35 a gallon.

When that time comes Ruben said, I'm walking!

 After dinner Ruben headed back to the office to see if he had any messages. It was still kind of early, 9:45 PM, depending on his messages he thought that he could still get a few things done. Maybe he'll call Ella and see if she completed that list. In the office he set down at his desk and checked his messages. Reached in the bottom desk drawer and pull out the bottle of Jim Bean, poured two fingers in his coffee cup and took a sip.

 Dolores call, said she was sorry about not wanting to see him again, she was a little upset. Call her! I met Dolores on my last case, two weeks after the case was over we were still doing it. I must call her the minute I get time.

Ella call, said she thought of something else, don't know if it'll shed any light on Richards's death but it's all she has right now.

The last time I saw Ella and the good doctor together was something like a year ago when I was going through that Tonelli thing, I happen to be in an out of the way lounge and ran into

them. I was sitting over in a corner alone, they didn't see me. As I said before we had both gone our separate ways but for some reason we were still living together. It wasn't an every night thing because she was home for four mornings out of the week, I'm guessing now because when she was home I wasn't. So it had to be a sexual thing, it was for me anyway. That is until I met Freda. I kind of fell for her. So that tells me if he was only with Ella two nights a week how does he spend the

rest of his

time? Bowling, Golf or going to the gym? Those are

things I have to look into. Maybe Raymond will come

up with something. If nothing else he will pass the word

around that I'm looking for information on the good

doctor. The phone rang and it was Ella, I was hoping

I'd catch you at the office Ella said.

I got your message but I thought it was a little late to

call, you still up Ruben said.

I couldn't sleep, have you come up with anything yet?

Ella, it's only been a few hours, I'm good but this is

going to take some time. I did go over to your friend's

apartment, looked around. Ran into a detective I knew,

I think I know more than him except for a suspect and

they have you for that. They may not look that much

further.

Do you think there is a chance of finding the real killer Ruben?

There's always a chance Ella but you have to give me time, I'm working on it.

Are you coming home tonight? Ella asked. I don't think so Ella, I get more of my thinking done here at the office. Besides I may hit the streets later on. You called earlier what had you remembered? Ruben said.

Richard was getting a lot of calls when we first started dating at all times of the night. And now that I think about it they were all men. Never a woman, not one time. That's strange.

Yes it is, especially for a single man, I'll look into it Ruben said. Is that it?

Yes, I thought you should know that, Ella said.

Ella, try not to worry, things will work themselves out.

At 11:30 PM it was still kind of early for what I do so I decided to head out for the cave club. That's always been a good place to find out things. Monday night they probably have a local live jazz band there. The club was packed almost like it was on a weekend. I paid the dollar fifty cover charge and walked in. They did have a local band playing and I had heard them before, they're not bad.

The Lords of Jazz, sax, trumpet, piano, bass and drums. There was a number of people I knew and I waved, shook hands, and kissed the ladies. Walked over to the bar and ordered a JB over ice. The bar was full, only a few seats left, mostly women. But a good number of men. Since it was the girl's night out.

RK is that you? Haven't seen you in at least five years. How you been?

The person that was speaking to me was named Nicky, he was another of the guys from the old neighborhood. He was always one of the coolest of the group, never got into our gang, or club like we used to call it. But was an associate you might say. Quiet guy and fairly good-looking, never had any trouble getting the girls like the rest of us. But he did his dirt just like the rest of us even theo he was the son of the local preacher man.

Hey Nicky, you the last person I expect to find in here especially on a Monday night. You still married?

Yeah, still married to Joyce RK, and I wouldn't be here if it wasn't for her boss getting wasted the other night and the cops telling her she should stick around town. We would be in Detroit visiting my mom about now.

Nicky, your wife's boss wouldn't happen to have been Richard Denton, the dentist would it?

Yeah, that's him. Was he your doctor to? No, but I am investigating his murder, any chance I could talk to her about it?

Yeah, I guess so RK, you still into that detective shit? Seems like I'm not good for anything else Nicky, when do you think I could talk to her? Ruben said.

Why don't you come by the house tomorrow, say about one? We're staying in my parent's old place, the old man passed away a few years ago and my mom moved to Detroit to live with her sister.

Nicky and I had a few more drinks together, caught up on old times and closed the place at 2 AM.

TUESDAY 8:45 AM

Rita woke me up where I was sleeping on the couch in the lounge.

RK, you here on the couch again, I think you should move in.

And good morning to you Rita, while you doing all this talking you could be making the coffee.

Right on it RK, Rita said.

Ruben got up went into the restroom and washed up, change his shirt and walked over to his desk, sat down and put his feet up and reach for the cup of coffee Rita had put down. Took a sip and found something was missing, reached in the bottom desk drawer and pull out what was left of his bottle of Jim Bean. Rita! I'm about out of JB, when the store opens would you go down and pick me up a couple bottles?

No! I will not. I was not hired on to fetch your liquor for you. Plus you haven't paid me for the last bottle.

Now Rita you know I'm not worth a dime until I get my morning nip, please!

Okay, okay, RK. But I want my money this time! The phone rang and Rita picked it up, Ruben Kane Detective agency, Rita speaking. Oh hi Raymond, yes he's here. RK, Raymond is on line 1.

Yeah Raymond, Any news? Ruben said.

Hey RK, you got another phone in your office now? What's with this line 1 stuff? It's a long story Raymond, what you got? You are paying for this information I'm giving you aren't you? Raymond said.

I got to get paid something.

Don't I always take care of you Raymond, now tell me what you got.

One of the guys came by the shop and started talking about the good doctor, you know he's in the paper now, picture and all. Well, he says he knows him or knows of him. Says he used to live on the east side and the old boy used to be kind of sweet, if you know what I mean. He left for dentistry school in the early 30s and never came back. Last anyone heard he had opened a dental office over on the west side, they say he's doing pretty well. Oh, and he says the cops has a suspect but they didn't say who.

Is that it Raymond? Ruben said.

Yeah, if I hear of anything else I'll let you know.

Good deal, and I'll take care of you the next time I'm on that side of town.

So the good doctor was a fairy, I'm sure Ella didn't know that, seems like the old boy was going both ways. That would explain why only men were calling his place. Ella was just for show. Well, that opens the door

for other suspects. Nicky's old lady (Joyce) should be
able to shed more light on things.

Tuesday 11:30 AM

There is on old railroad car that was made into a diner
in downtown Cleveland so I went there for lunch. Good
food and cheap prices, that's what I'm talking bout. I
needed something to fill that hole the liquor had eaten
through my gut the night before, if I didn't know any
better one would say I'm an alcoholic but that can't be
true because I can stop drinking any time I won't (Says
the drunk to the Pope). After lunch I headed for
Nicky's on the east side, on the way I stopped by
Raymond's to pay him that little change I owe him.
 Nicky's parents place looked the same, don't look like
he did much improvement to the place, it brought back
old memories. Like smoking pot and drinking wine in

the garage, pulling trains on girls, what a time! Nicky's wife Joyce was one of those girls we pulled a train on but he married her anyway. What the hell was he thinking? I remember we never brought it up ever again, we just looked at each other. Although it's not like we stayed in each other's face, each went their separate ways. And I guess she made him a good wife, they've been married a number of years now and until the other night I hadn't seen him in some years and I'm out all the time. Oh well, good for them. I parked in front of the house and walked up the walkway and up the few steps to the door, knocked a few times and waited. After a minute or so Nicky came to the door.

 Hey RK, right on time. Joyce is in the back yard in the garden, I'll get her. Have a seat. You feeling all right after last night I asked?

No I'm not RK, I can't hang like I used to, I'll be right back.

After a few minutes

Joyce walked in wearing a pair of old bib overalls, dirt on the knees and a plaid shirt. Baseball cap over a due rag and rubber boots. She was looking rough. But take all that away and I could tell that she was still cute as could be. Even after three kids. I remember her back in the day, 5 feet 2 with short curly black hair, boyish build, cute as hell and would go for just about anything.

Hi RK, haven't seen you in years, how you been? Have you seen any of the old gang lately?

I had gotten up and walked over to her to give her a hug even though she looked the way she did but what do you do with old friends you haven't seen in years.

She tried to stop me with; No! RK don't do that, I'm a mess. I hugged her anyway.

After that was done we caught up on old times. What I've been doing, moved to the west side years ago I told her. I see the   gang from time to time, I still get around because that's my job but I'm just not over on this side of town much anymore I said.

As you know most everyone has moved away from here but us, we're still here she said. But we do read about you every now and then RK, like last year when Tonelli and Bullet were killed.

Yeah, well they tried to drag me into all that but the lady I was working for cleared all that up, her and her lawyers that is.

Joyce, Nicky tells me you worked for Richard Denton? In what capacity and for how long did you work for him?

Nicky told me you were investigating Dr. Denton's death, how do you know him she asked?

Oh, friend of a friend asked me to look into his death I said. You were saying, how long you had worked for him and what job you held.

I was the office manager and worked for him for four years. Joyce said.

Did he have any problems there, like people owing him money and not paying, things like that?

Yes, well that's the nature of a dental practice. You always have someone owing money but no one would kill him over it.

Who else worked there beside you? I said.

Two dental assistance, we sent a lot of work out, Joyce said.

Have you noticed anything out the ordinary happening around the office that you could think of, girlfriends bugging him, jealous husbands, anything like that?

No, I don't know of anything like that but I did hear he had a girlfriend but I never saw her. Before that only men would call but I assume they were all patients or country club members. After the girlfriend came along the calls from men kind of cut back.

Was he one to go out a lot, and if so where did he go? Ruben asked.

I wasn't into his business like that even though I was the office manager, but I do remember once receiving a call from the Rainbow room confirming a reservation. The Rainbow room is an upscale restaurant/club on the west side of town near the water she said. Not many of us go there maybe because of money but the ones of us that has money are there, Joyce said.

Would you say that the good doctor was one of those that has that kind of money? I said. You got that right RK, Dr. Denton had a hell of a practice going on, and money was no problem for him. I don't know where I'm going to find another job like that. Poor Dr. Denton!

What's going to happen to the practice now that he's gone, Ruben said.

Hopefully another Dentist will come in but that still don't mean he'll keep me and the others, they usually bring in their own people Joyce said.

Well, thanks Joyce for enlightening me about the good doctor if you think of anything else would you let me know, and I got up to leave and gave her one of my cards.

I will RK, and don't be a stranger we are here most days, when we're not running with the kids.

Nicky came from outback and we said our goodbyes and promised to keep in touch and I headed out wondering what my next stop would be.

CHAPTER 3

3:45 PM, I was walking into my office and Rita was on her way out. We had no set time for her to be there or when to leave just a reasonable time for both.

Any calls Rita?

There're on your desk RK. I have to run, got an appointment at the hairdresser. I'm her last client of the day so I have to hurry, see you tomorrow. And oh yeah, I picked up your whiskey and took my money out of the petty cash box.

After Rita left I walked into my office threw my hat at the hat rack, missed and continued on to my desk, took my coat off put it on the back of the chair. Set down and checked out my messages.

The first message was from my policy man (Bernie). RK, that number you played last night, 456, came out. I'm holding 125 big ones for you. I'll play the same number again if I don't hear from you, there're known to double back you know. Let me know!

The second message was from a fellow named Ralph, he says he has information on Dr. Denton; I hear you're paying. My number is Wabash 2387.

I reached in the bottom desk drawer and pulled out a brand-new bottle of Jim Bean, bust the cap and poured two fingers in my coffee cup. After knocking that out I decided to call this Ralph guy maybe he can add something to the good doctor's murder.

Ralph this is Ruben Kane, you called me?

I did Mr. Kane, I have information for you but first

how much is it worth to you?

Depends Ralph on the information.

Okay Mr. Kane I'll tell you what, I'll tell you what I

know then you tell me what it's worth to you, what

about that?

I'll go with that, shoot!

I've known Richard Denton for many years and we had

a relationship up until about a year ago then he cut it

off. I'm not naïve, I know that he's had other affairs

during the time we were together but I just looked the

other way. This time a woman was involved and he

asked me to move out, we were living together. He says

he found someone else so I moved out. I'm thinking it's

another male but I was wrong, this time it was a

female, I wasn't ready for that. As long as I've been

knowing him he's never had a relationship with a woman, that I know of that is.

Ralph, who do you think would want to kill him, any ideas?

Mr. Kane I think if he was out there running from this one and that it could have been just about anyone. He still hang out at this one club we all go to, check it out it's called the Boomerang club in downtown Cleveland. I've heard of it I said.

I thanked Ralph and told him to stop by the office and my secretary would have a 20 spot waiting for him. Wednesday, 6:15 PM. I started getting those hunger pains again and wondering what I had a taste for, something light! Mama Sues and fried chicken, cabbage and okra, red beans and homemade rolls. Maybe apple pie on the side with coffee. The only thing wrong with that is no nip to put in the coffee. I'm going to have to start carrying me a flask around with me.

An hour later I was headed for the house to see if Ella had come up with anything new. When I walked in the door she was sitting at the kitchen table nursing a filth of Mr. Ben's Gin that was a quarter gone. What are you doing I said, trying to drink your problems away?

She looked at me all sad and said, I wish it was so but this Gin don't seem to be doing it for me. Where have you been she said?

Oh, here and there, seeing what I could turn over I said.

And did you, turn over anything Ella asked?

Some I said, how you coming on that list, that would help.

I went back to where we first met in the grocery store to where he took me on our first date, to who we met, till I left to pick up the drinks. Here, see for yourself. I looked over the list and one of the places that caught my attention was the Rainbow room that Joyce had told me about, but no Boomerang club. I guess I wouldn't since that's an all-male bar/club, and he show-nuff wouldn't take her there. I didn't see it and I didn't mention it.

Will that help she said?

Everything helps I said.

What about the items I left at the apartment? She said.

The cops has them I said, besides they already know that you and he were having an affair and right now you are there only suspect. What we need to come up with is someone else that would have a reason to kill him. I walked over to the kitchen cabinet and pulled

out my bottle of Jim Bean, might as well!

Are you going back out Ella asked?

I am, nothing I can do around here and the only

suspect here is you, I said.

Ruben, I did not kill Richard, want you believe me?

Ella, did you know Richard was funny?

What do you mean Ruben, funny! As in a comic book

funny?

No! Sweet, a fairy, walked on the wild side, went both

ways, "A PUNK" I eventually said.

She had her drink in her hand and dropped it and

stood up and stared at me, fists clenched.

You are a liar Ruben, you take that back, she

screamed.

Hey don't get mad at me I'm just the messenger. After a year or however long it was you were going together you should have known.

I don't believe you Ruben and even if he were I would have known, how do you know that any way she asked?

Ella, I am a detective you know. I'm only telling you this because if I know then the cops know. And if you say or tell them you didn't know then there going to won't to know why not. You're already near

the top of their list now, where do you think that little bit of information is going to put you?

When I left the apartment Ella really dived into the bottle then, maybe I shouldn't have said anything about the good doctor but she would have found out sooner or later, better hearing it from me.

There is no getting around it I have to make a trip to the boomerang room.

The boomerang club was set on a backstreet, so small that a car couldn't squeeze through, the street was only wide enough for bicycles and pedestrian traffic. Kind of remind you of the streets in Europe, so I've been told and the pictures I've seen. Even the streets were Copper stone. I parked the Buick on the street just before the Boomerang passage, five cars down and just set and watch the area to see who comes and goes. All men! No! There's a woman. About 5 feet eight, 150 or hundred and 60 pounds, large felt hat and face that wasn't that bad. Kind of cute. The boobs were there but the waist was kind of thick and the legs in a short skirt was let's call them, odd. I leaned over the steering wheel to see if I could get a better look and I said out loud; woman my ass, that's a man. Well, here I go. I closed and locked the door on the Buick, Walked down to the passage going down to the club, met up with a couple other men who were going that way and continued up to the club. Two of the men were walking side-by-side the third walked beside me and said. I haven't seen you here before, this your first time? It sure is Ruben said. How about you? Oh I'm a regular, I'm here at least twice a week.

This place is kind of hard to find Ruben said. I've lived in Cleveland all my life and it was hard for me to find. Let me guess, you're straight he said? You're right Ruben said. How could you tell? There are ways he said. I'm here investigating the death of Dr. Richard Denton, did you know him? Richard, sure I knew him he was a regular here to. By that time we had reach the entrance way approximately 3 Quarters Way down the block with a dead end at the other end. The marquee said boomerang, with the picture of same in the left upper corner, lights flashing. We had to walk downstairs to get in the place, right at the bottom of the stairs was the bar spanning the length of the club. Tables all around but not too close together. Jukebox, 3 to 4 private rooms to the side, at the other end of the club was on exit sign and rest room area. The fellow I was with said, let's sit over there. It was near one of the private rooms. The waitress or waiter came over (should have guessed) and took our order. Look, I'm just as open minded as the next guy but I'm used to my waitresses having a short skirt, nice legs and big breasts, this person had neither. He or she was in between man and woman, but I was cool. Jim Bean over ice I said, my friend ordered Rum and Coke. I'm Ronnie he says, and you would be? Ruben I said. I didn't give my last name because he didn't give me his. You say you're looking into Richard's death? You some kind of cop or something Ronnie said. More like a private detective I said. I thought the police already had a suspect in custody, Are you saying that's not so? Cops, what do they know, most have tunnel vision, most of the time anyway I said. But you don't believe they have the right person do you or you wouldn't be around here asking questions now would you, Ronnie said. I don't think people around here will go for that. You are giving me all my answers without me asking one question, I said. Maybe you should be the detective. Let me ask you this, how long did you know him? I said. Oh I didn't, I just seen him around the club but we never got together, if you know what I mean. By the time I was headed his way someone had beat me to him. He was that popular I said? That's right he said. A poor queen like me, I didn't stand a chance. Did he happen to have a girlfriend, I don't see any ladies in here. You won't unless they come in as guests and you probably couldn't tell the difference. They have their place and we have ours, everybody happy. I don't think he had a girlfriend that's frowned on around here but some do but keep it under cover. Did Richard have a study? Yeah, matter of fact he did. You see that fellow sitting at the bar, the far end of the bar. I seen him with

Richard a number of times, don't know his name. Ruben are you sure you're not one of us? If so we could get something going right now. If not the night is wasting away and quite frankly I'm looking to get laid tonight. I assured Ronnie I was not one of them. So without further ado I'll be moving along, he said. I thanked Ronnie and call the waiter or waitress over and ordered another drink. I had one sent over to the guy at the bar that Ronnie had pointed out to me. When the drink was delivered to him he turned around to see where it came from and the waiter/waitress pointed me out. He tipped his glass to me in a thank you gesture, got up and started walking my way. Halfway across the room two men stood up and stopped him and told him something that Ruben couldn't hear but he turned around and went back to the bar and his seat. The men both of average height smaller than me anyway, sat down at my table and one said Kane! That your name? No need to answer we know who you are. Now, Richard was a good man and we don't want his name drug into the dirt so we're asking you, stop! What you're doing. The police has their suspect, let's leave it at that. Do we understand each other? He said. You may understand I said but I'm needing more answers. You have gotten as much information from here as you're gonna get, now it's time for you to leave. Well fellows I really wasn't ready to leave and before I got out leave! I was hit, not just any hit but one that shook me right down to my toes, before I hit the floor another blow came to the other side of my head. Somewhere a number three showed up behind me and started helping the other two. One on one I could have held my own, one against two 50-50 maybe but three, no chance. I woke up in a back alley, somewhere. Behind the club I'm guessing. Head hurting, ribs I think may be broke along with my nose. I pulled myself up against the dumpster I was lying beside and held my head, and just sat there. A black cat came from around the dumper and walked across my legs and looked back at me and walked on down the alley. I must be getting close to something but I'll be damn if I know what. Look like Ella is being join on the suspect list. I looked at my watch and saw it was 2:45 AM, I've been in this alley approximately three hours. I checked for my wallet, and keys to the Buick. They were all there. Let me find out exactly where I am. I walked out the alley or should I say crawled out, spotted my car and made a beeline for it. The street was empty at this time of mourning and my vehicle was the only one in sight.

I walked in my office and to my desk, pulled out my bottle and took me a long hit right out of the jug. Took the bottle with my coffee cup and went back to the lounge and the couch. Took my hat and put it on the chair, took my sport coat off and rolled it up and put it behind my head. Poured four fingers of JB and tried to relax for the first time in a while that's when everything went black.

RK, you here again, do you ever go home? Rita said. Oh my Lord look at your face, what happened to you?

And good morning to you Rita, could you by any chance make some coffee? What time is it? 9:45 AM Rita said. Do you need to know what day it is also? No! I'm sure I know that. What day is it? He said. Thursday, Rita said. I think you need to see a doctor. I'll be fine, just the coffee and a sip of JB and I'll be as good as new. I walked into the bathroom, look in the mirror and saw what Rita saw, I was a mess. Left eye partly closed, huge knot on my forehead, Nose was bent kind of funny. Lips was split in two places. Felt like one of my back tooth was loose. Ribs felt none to good nether. Change my shirt and transferred my suspenders to my last pair of pants. I checked my sport coat and found it wasn't in too bad a shape, my fedora was beat up some but since it wasn't cheap it bounced right back into shape. I can't take another ass kicking like that one for sure, so I went to my desk and took out the 38. Check the chamber and saw that it was ready to go. That's my last ass kicking this year, if I can help it. I haven't had a beat down like that since bullet and I got into it. The phone rang and Rita picked it up, yes he's here, she said. Mr. Kane a Mr. Seymour is on line one. Hello, I said.

Ruben Kane? This is Seymour Johnson, I was in the club last night. I'm sorry what happened to you but there was nothing I could do. And who would you be I asked. I'm the guy who was sitting at the end of the bar that you bought a drink for, I started over to your table but got persuaded not to. You want to tell me who were those fellows that asked me to leave the club so nicely, I said? They are what we call the peacekeepers, they keep things quiet so nothing or no one gets out of hand. They knew who you were as soon as you walked in. So why this call Seymour, I know it's not because you're concerned about my health. Well yes and no Mr. Kane, I knew they wouldn't kill you they just wanted to get your attention. Well that's good to hear because I could swear they were trying to kill me I said. So what can I do for you Seymour? I hear you are looking into the death of Richard and I wanted to help. I was involved with Richard until his latest came along, it was news to me when I found out it was a woman. I didn't think he went that way. So you are telling me you don't believe she killed him? I don't know, I'm not sure. When I was with him I knew he went behind my back more than a few times. What have you been hearing around the club, I know they've been talking? Everybody's baffled, but everyone loved him. So what are they afraid of I said. I'm just trying to find out the truth. The truth may come back to hurt the club and we can't have that, there is only so many places we can go and if for some reason the club gets closed down, well you can see where I'm going with this. We all love Richard but not enough to see the club close. What about you Seymour, did you love him enough to kill him, you had good reason. He did cut you loose for a woman. No way man, too many fish out there for me to knock him off, besides he was my meal ticket. There was at least three or four others hitting that and they wasn't all regulars at the club. Check out Dr. Stephen Boyd at the Cleveland clinic. Married, big house in the suburbs, grown kids and a yacht, that sort of thing. I followed Richard out there one weekend and witnessed them meet up. No wife, no kids, no guest, just Theo's two. That went on I think until the day of his death, so I'm thinking if he cut him loose along with me the good doctor didn't like it and knocked him off. Could have happened that way. Yeah, I thought to myself. And the list gets longer.

Well thanks Seymour I'll sure look into this Dr. Boyd. You will keep me informed if you hear of anything further at the club? He said he would and hung up.

CHAPTER 4

There were times when I drove through the hood at night especially and came across a few teenagers standing on the corner singing, sometimes I would even stop and listen. No music just harmonizing, sounded damn good. They should have put a few of those sounds on vinyl. A number of them were made up, I've never heard them before but then again I wouldn't since I'm quite a bit older than them. Who ever heard of "Annie had a baby, can't work no more" society would never go for that. Or "work with me Henry". Sounded good and even had me tapping my feet. Then I would hear the bass kick in with, DD bone, Debone, bone, debone. And then the baritone with the same tune only a little higher came in. Second tenor with a higher version of the same tune and the lead singer told the bass (little bit) bring that bass out a little louder. Yeah, that's it. Bug man, keep it right there, you sounding good.

Baritone drop-down a little, yeah, we doing it now. Bass, baritone and second Tenor blend there Individual voices together in one soul sounding tone. Debone, debone, debone, bone bone. And repeated. Then the lead singer started singing. "Getting on down to see my woman, getting on down to see my girl, She lives in Charlotte, North Carolina, right by the Golden spear motel. Greyhound bus is going there tomorrow all I need is seven bucks for the fare, and in 24 hours I'll be pulling right on in there". Bomb DD boom debone, debone.

The next day I headed for Dr. Boyd's house, I had called him a little earlier to make on appointment I explain who I was and what I wanted to discuss, Richard's death, and to my surprise he said he'd be happy to. Driving through his neighborhood just west of Cleveland you could see the money right there on the water. Two and three story homes spaced on 5 acres or more of land. Curve driveways with the latest automobiles in front. Some with boat ramps in the back, now that was living. I pulled in the circle in front of a colonial three-story home with double front doors, a doorknob made in the form of a Buffalo. I knocked on the door three times before anyone answered. The Butler that came to the door was dressed as the typical Asian Butler would be, black suit, white shirt with bowtie. Clean-shaven, I said, Mr. Kane for Dr. Boyd. I have an appointment. Please come in the Butler said

Dr. Boyd is expecting you. Dr. Boyd is in the library, right this way. May I take your hat? I gave him my hat not because I wanted to but because in this type of environment I just felt it call for it. I walked in the library which was about the size of my apartment. Books covering three sides of the room with what look like original paintings in between. Like van Gogh and the such, you know what I'm talking bout. A full bar with a large mirror behind and many bottles of liquor. I even spotted my brand (Jim Bean) in the mix. Mr. Boyd or Dr. Boyd was a small white man of about 5 foot two, small hands, head half bald and wearing white slacks and white silk button-down shirt. He had that confidence that all doctors seem to have and even though his size was small he had the appearance of a very large person. Mr. Kane he said, you wanted to talk to me about Richard? I was sorry to hear about him,

very sorry. May I offer you something to drink?

Of course I said yes, just a small one. JB and rocks. How well did you know him Dr. Boyd? Oh I've been knowing Richard for some years now. He had not too long gotten out of dental school and we met at the country club on the golf course. What kind of relationship did you two have if I may ask? You do get straight to the point don't you Mr. Kane. I'm gonna assume that you know something about Richard and I before you came here, so here it is. Richard and I had a relationship for many years but it wasn't exclusive, I know he had others but when I call he would always be there. How did that interfere with your home life I asked him? My wife always knew about me and the kids are hers so I don't feel I owe them anything. You could say that we have an arrangement that benefit both of us. That's nice work if you can get it, I said. How did you feel about Richard? I loved Richard in my own way but I didn't kill him that's why I agreed to speak to you. I want you to find out who killed him. Then you don't believe the suspect they have did it? No! I mean I really don't know. Did you know that it is a woman that's suspected of killing him? I heard that but something just don't feel right about her being the one. I could be wrong he said. Nevertheless I'm willing to pay you to find out who did. Well Dr. Boyd I accept your offer but I must say this. I go where the evidence takes me, regardless of who it is, do you understand what I'm saying Dr. Boyd? I do, Boyd said.

By the time I left Boyd's residence I was convinced he had nothing to do with Richard's death, him paying me could have had something to do with that. Hell, someone should pay me. $300 wasn't bad for an afternoons work. Later on I did check out his whereabouts the night of Richard's death and he was where he said he was and that was the country club with his wife. Just for the hell of it I went to the liquor store Ella went to for the alcohol for her and Richard. I know it's kind of like saying I didn't trust my wife but you have to cover all bases. Plus' she don't have to know. The clerk that was on duty happen to be working the night of the killing and remembered Ella. Even what she purchased, two fifths of gin and two quarts of tonic water. I asked him did he noticed anything in particular about her that night. He said no, when I tried to joke with her she never fell for it. I mean she didn't smile or nothing and most people at least smile at my jokes. She just looked at me deadpan, paid for the purchase and got into her car and left. Wait a minute, got into her car? She wasn't walking? No, she wasn't walking because I saw her drive up and you know I watched her walk away. If you ever saw her you do know she has a nice ass, so I watched her walk away.

Did you tell this to the police? No, I never spoke to the police, you're the only one who's been around asking questions. I thanked the clerk and left. Well, I'll be damn. I thought she walked, that's what she told me. She lied, she lied. Driving versus walking that knocks off 10 to 15 minutes from the time she says it took her to walk. You can do a lot in 15 minutes, even set up a killing. I can't believe that, I won't believe that. Ella couldn't kill anybody.

Back at the office I received a phone call. Ruben, this is Detective Jeffries I haven't heard from you, what have you come up with, anything or do we proceed with prosecuting Ella. Not much detective Jeffries, and he went on to tell him about getting his head bashed in at the Boomerang club and meeting Dr. Boyd but not telling him about the liquor store clerk, let him find out for himself. You know Ruben he said, there could be a case made about you. Ella being your wife and all. You finding out she and he were seeing each other, you getting jealous and killing the old boy. I'm just saying, Jeffrey said. Well, say all you like, I didn't kill him and neither did Ella.

Shortly our investigation will be complete and we'll be handing it over to the district attorney that is if we don't come up with any other suspects. I'm just giving you a heads up so if you have anything, I'd pick up my pace if I were you. Do you understand me Ruben?

I hear you, Ruben said. Once they indict Ella they may pull her bail then the heat will really be on. Either I have to come up with the real killer or come up with a scapegoat. Hey! That's just the way it is.

The boomerang club, I really hated to go back there but it looked like I have no choice, I have nowhere else to go. Things will be different this time, I hope! Somebody's gonna tell me something.

CHAPTER 5

11 o'clock that night I parked on the same street, walked down the same passage way and walked down the same flight of stairs. The bar was partly filled on this night, I took a table this time with my back against the wall. The same"barmaid"came over to me and said, I didn't think I'd see you back here again so soon. I said, the place just grows on me I guess. JB on the rocks please. Two of the old boys that jump me were on the other side of the room sitting at a table looking in my direction but I didn't see number three. I knew there was a number three, I just never saw him but I had smelled him. His cologne, smelled like a piece of dried up fruit, I couldn't forget that. Ronnie came out of one of the back rooms with a fellow I hadn't seen before, went over to the table where old boys were sitting and turned around and looked my way. Ronnie and friend came walking towards me and said, you

back? I stood up and said after shaking his hand, can't stay away. This is my assistant he said mentioning toward his shadow. I reached out to shake his hand and after doing so touched my nose as Theo I had an etch. He smelled just like a dead or dried up piece of fruit. I think I just found old boy number three. The "barmaid" arrived with my drink and I asked Ronnie and friend could I buy them a drink. I don't think you gonna have time for another drink old boy said, you may not even have time to finish the one you have. Since Mr. Kane has taken the time to return to the boomerang after what happened to him the last time let him have his say Ronnie said. Ronnie pointed over to the next table and old boy sat there. Ronnie set with me. Now, Mr. Kane, what is it? You never told me last time we met that you were such a big wheel around here Ruben said. How did you find out, it's not very well known Ronnie said? Right after you left the table last time I was here that was when old boys came over to harass me, after thinking about it I knew it had to be you who sent them, since I talked to no one else but you. What is it you don't want me to find out? Were you screwing Richard too? No! I'm sorry to tell you this but I don't go that way. Just because I'm part owner in a place like this don't mean I have to indulge. So everything you told me last time we met was a lie? I told you what you wanted to hear, he said. I took a shot in the dark and said, how much of a percentage did Richard have in the club? Ronnie raised his eyes at that and just looked at me and said, a third. And who controls the other third? I can't tell you that he said. So the two that's left have a third to split between themselves, that could be calls to kill him right there. I didn't kill him and neither did any of my employees, you'll have to look somewhere else. Your employees are surely capable of killing someone, they did a good job on me. I'll assure you Mr. Kane if they wanted to kill you they would have. Now, your time is up and I must ask you to leave or do you need help? Gap, help Mr. Kane to the exit door.

Let's go Kane, gap said. But I haven't finish my drink yet. Let's go, gap said again. Well, if I must. I stood up and thanked Ronnie for his help and started toward the front door. Not that way gap said, and pointed me toward the rear exit. Are you sure, I said? Move, gap said. We cross the room to the rear exit passing the two old boys who helped me out the last time, as we were going through the exit door I noticed them getting up that's when I turned around with the 38 in hand and slap gap upside the head. The door closed behind us and I slapped him three more times while he was falling toward the ground and putting a lot of feeling in the blows then I took off running. Halfway down the alley the exit door open and the other two came out. That's when I turned the corner and headed for my ride. One out of three ain't bad, I'll settle for that.

RK, Mr. Loft is on line 1, Rita said.

Ruben guess what? Your license finally came through, even though you been going under the radar for over a year now without them, even got your weapons license back for you. I'll send it over by carrier, I know you need it. Course it never stopped you from doing what you do anyway.

That is some good news Loft but for what they charge me I could have done without them. Until you got caught, thank your lucky stars and move on Loft said. Anything new going on with Ella's case? I said. I should be asking you that, you're out there in the street, Loft said. Have you come up with anything? I know the cops haven't or they would have called me, or the DA would have. But I'll tell you right now, they're happy, because they have Ella, there're not going to look very hard for someone else, Loft said. I'm out here trying the best I can loft, something will break.

I hope so Ruben, if not I'd start looking for another wife. After loft hung up I received another call from a Mr. Seymour. Mr. Kane this is Seymour you said to call you if anything happened here at the club I mean other than what happened the other night with Gap. You know he's in the hospital. No I didn't, that's too bad. They say he'll be laid up for at least a week. But that's not what I call you about, a fellow came in the club this afternoon that I hadn't seen before except in the newspaper. He's a doctor that works at the Cleveland clinic. Little guy, about 5 foot two or so, 110 or 20 pounds. He met up with Ronnie and they went in one of the back rooms, stayed about 30 minutes and he left. Do you have any idea what they talked about I said. I'm afraid not Mr. Kane business I would imagine. That sounds good Seymore, anything else? No, that's it for now. We've been getting a lot of traffic around here the last week or so. I feel like they're about to sale the place. Seymour you seem to be at the club quite a bit, you work there are something? Didn't I tell you, I'm the clubs custodian? I may be here anytime. I'll talk to you later Mr. Kane. So Dr. Boyd is the third investor, he didn't mention that. It looks like the good doctor was taking business with pleasure, and hiring me I think was just a way to find out what I knew and keeping tabs on me. Dr. Boyd is one sneaky mother jumper.

I know the cops have probably covered it but I had a hunch that I should check out the alley behind Richard's apartment. Never can tell, they may have missed something. They never did find the gun.

I started at the beginning of the alley right behind the apartment it being right on the corner. And worked up from there, checked garbage cans, dumpsters, behind bushes, old cars and signs. Telephone poles and everyplace else I could think of. I walked up one side and down the other, then I decided to hit the next alley on the next block, nothing. Although people were looking out their windows wondering what I was doing, thought I was scavenging for food I guess. In this neighborhood you don't see too many people doing that, none I would guess. After spending two hours doing that I decided to give it up, look like I'll have to change cloths again. On the way back to my car I noticed a little kid of about eight years old playing with a toy pistol or what I thought was a toy Pistol until I stopped and took a closer look. The kid pointed the weapon at me and went Bam! Bam! Bam! And I said, what the hell. That look like a real gun. Hey kid, I said. Let me take a look at that. I don't know the kid said, you gonna give it back? Sure, I'll give it back to you. He gave me the gun with some effort because of its weight. A 38 Smith and Wesson, what you know about that, looks like mine. Where'd you get this I asked? I found it in the alley on the next block he said. Did it happen to be near that large apartment building? A couple of buildings down from there he said that's where the lady throw it. My mouth dropped open and I stared at him and asked, what did you just say? What lady? The lady, I watched throw it in the bushes and after she left I went and got it. One other thing I said. What did this lady look like? He described Ella to a Tee. I paid the kid five dollars for the gun, him saying something about buying a two holster set like Hopalong Cassidy.

What to do, what to do. Looks like the cops have got the right person after all, now what are you going to do about it I said to myself. She did put on a good show, damn show fooled me. And I've been married to her for over five years. Ruben, I didn't kill him, Ruben I'm not the one, Ruben why don't you believe me. A mother jumper! Lied all the time.

That night I was at the Worms lounge, a small out of the way place that I thought hardly anyone knew about but I found out that most everyone knew about. I use to bring a lady or two here to so-called get away from the crowds. Nice quiet and intimate, small tables for two, candles on the tables and soft music piped in over the hidden speakers. I took my usual table over in the corner and ordered my favorite drink, JB on the rocks. I thought this would be the perfect place to think about what I should do. Directly across the room from me at another small table was where I first saw Ella and Richard almost a year ago.

They never saw me and I was surprised to see them, they did seem to be in love at that time, even I could see that clear across the room. I had Freda at the time but I still found myself getting a little jealous. Nevertheless, she killed Richard and I believe I know why. She found out he was a punk and couldn't handle it or he was going to dump her and go back to his old ways. After all he did dump Seymour, Ralph and Boyd for her so why not the other way around. She lied to me from the start, I could see her lying to the police even our lawyer and bondsman, but not to me.Not me! Even though we been going our separate ways for close to a year now there has to be something there. I was wrong about one thing, she is capable of murder. Maybe I should have been sleeping with one eye open. Still when she got in trouble she came to me. The gun, I have it. And I'll bet it still has her prints on it. She was probably in such a rush getting rid of it she forgot about wiping it clean. The only thing I haven't figured out is did she kill him before or after she went to the liquor store. My guess is before, that way she could get rid of the gun on the way there or coming back. One, driving to the store instead of walking. Two, talking to the store clerk. Three, the kid in the alley and finding the gun. If they knew all that, they'd have my poor wife by her short Hairs. But I don't think the cops are that smart, they think they have Ella so they're not going to look any further or gather anymore evidence. I called the waitress over and ordered another drink, a double. I finally made up my mind to what I was going to do.

Epilogue

Two weeks later Ella and Ruben were sitting at the kitchen table having their morning coffee and reading the paper. Ella was reading the main part and Ruben had the sports section. The Cleveland Indians won a doublehiter last night he said, it's about time they got there shit together. I guess they'll lose the next five in a row now. Ella put her part of the paper down on the table and said to Ruben, tell me again how they found the killer of Richard? Hell Ella, you don't want to hear that story again do you, it should be enough that you're off the hook for it. Just once more and I promise to leave you alone she said.

Okay, okay. The police got an anonymous phone call that this guy at the boomerang club had kill Richard and he still had the gun in his apartment. They went over to his apartment after getting a search warrant and sure enough there was the gun right where the caller said it would be. Right in the back of his closet in a shoebox. They started checking and found out that Richard had found out that he was stealing from the club and was going to turn him in. Ronnie, that's the guy's name, said that the gun was planted and he didn't know where it came from or who did it. After they told him about his fingerprints being on the gun he says before the cops got there he found it and naturally picked it up. That's the only reason his prints were on the gun. Like they would believe that Ruben said. One day later you were released and here you are. That was some kind of luck, them finding that gun wasn't it Ruben? Who do you think drop that nickel on him? I have no idea Ella, can I go back to reading my paper now. I'll bet you'll believe me the next time when I tell you something want you Ruben? You'll never doubt me again will you Ruben? I think you owe me an apology, are you ready to apologize Ruben?

Ruben! Ruben!

End

Other Books by this Author

Enlisted at 14... A Memoir

Enlisted at 14...And the Journey Continues

Willow...A Novel

Just a Dream

Willow...and the Medusa

Enlisted at 14...Looking Back

Meet Ruben Kane

Willow ... One for the team

www.ingramcontent.com/pod-product-compliance
Lightning Source LLC
Chambersburg PA
CBHW071143250626
47159CB00006B/2274